All Year Round

Emilie Leduc

Translated by Shelley Tanaka

First published in French in 2012 as *La ronde des mois* by Les éditions de la courte échelle inc.

First published in English in Canada and the USA in 2015 by Groundwood Books

Groundwood Books / House of Anansi Press
110 Spadina Avenue, Suite 801, Toronto, Ontario M5V 2K4
or c/o Publishers Group West
1700 Fourth Street, Berkeley, CA 94710

We acknowledge for their financial support of our publishing program the Canada Council for the Arts, the Government of Canada through the Canada Book Fund (CBF) and the Ontario Arts Council.

Canada Council for the Arts · Conseil des Arts du Canada

ONTARIO ARTS COUNCIL
CONSEIL DES ARTS DE L'ONTARIO
an Ontario government agency
un organisme du gouvernement de l'Ontario

Library and Archives Canada Cataloguing in Publication
Leduc, Emilie
[Ronde des mois. English]
All year round / written and illustrated by Emilie Leduc ; translated by Shelley Tanaka.
Translation of: La ronde des mois.
Issued in print and electronic formats.
ISBN 978-1-55498-411-4 (bound). — ISBN 978-1-55498-412-1 (pdf)
I. Tanaka, Shelley, translator II. Title. III. Title: Ronde des mois. English
PS8623.E4265R6613 2015 jC843'.6 C2015-900288-5
C2015-900289-3

The illustrations were done in color pencils on Mylar paper.
Printed and bound in Malaysia

FSC
www.fsc.org
MIX
Paper from responsible sources
FSC® C012700

For Rose

January

I am a giant.
I tromp through the forest.
Crunch! Swoosh!

The wind sings me a nursery rhyme.

I love the month of January
and the forest so white.

February

All day long I guard my fort.
Boots, hat, coat — my suit of armor is frozen stiff!

I love the month of February
and my hot chocolate, too.

March

Confetti rains on my head.
I take a big breath and blow out my candles.

I love the month of March
and funny hats.

April

Mademoiselle Clementine
hides under the carpet.
A princess like you should
keep her coat nice and dry.

I love the month of April,
and so does my sweet tooth.

May

I say hello to the butterfly, and he tells me his secret.
He has tasted the sweetness of dew.
I wish I could, too.

I love the month of May
and the flowers with their bright colors.

June

I ride very, very fast
in my little race car.
Zoom right! Zoom left!
You'll never catch me!

I love the month of June
and racing around the track.

July

I am so light I can fly, but I have no wings!
The water tickles my hair.
I swim upside down, my toes in the air.

I love the month of July
and my skin all pruney.

August

The water stretches out to meet the sky.
The sun is happy to sink into it
and swim all night long to cool off,
like a big lazy fish.

I love the month of August
and the nice warm sand.

September

The wind teases the trees.
They laugh so hard that their leaves turn red and fall.
Now there is nowhere to hide!

I love the month of September
and the big piles of leaves.

October

And, boo!
With my little red nose
I am a magic clown.
I hide behind the pumpkins
and make Clementine jump.

I love the month of October
and crunchy caramels.

November

The snow drifts everywhere.
But beneath my feet lie hidden
treasures
in all the colors of the rainbow.

I love the month of November
and the gentle flakes of snow.

December

A kingdom all in white.
Tiny diamonds frozen on my nose.
It makes me shiver when I taste them.

I love the month of December
and the icy lakes.